THE MISANTHROPE

CELIMENE: No, I'd rather you believed it's to Oronte.
             It's *his* attentions that I really want.   *(Act II, p. 50)*

ALCESTE (Alec McCowen)   CELIMENE (Diana Rigg)

MOLIERE

THE
MISANTHROPE

Modern English Adaptation by

TONY HARRISON

THE THIRD PRESS
Joseph Okpaku Publishing Company, Inc.
444 Central Park West, New York, N.Y. 10025

Including photographs from the National Theatre Company premiere
production at London's Old Vic, 22 February 1973, with Diana Rigg
as Celimene and Alec McCowen as Alceste.

This play is fully protected by copyright and all
applications for performing rights should be
made to Fraser & Dunlop Scripts Ltd., 91 Regent
Street, London W1R8RU.

Library of Congress Catalog Card Number:
73-83157

SBN: 89388-112-0 clothbound
     89388-113-9 paperback

First printing

Designed by Bennie Arrington

Cover photo: Diana Rigg as Celimene and Alec McCowen as Alceste
in the National Theatre Company production.

JANE EYRE'S SISTER

This version of *Le Misanthrope* commissioned by the National Theatre for production in 1973, the tercentenary of Molière's death, sets the play in 1966, exactly three hundred years after its first performance. One of the focuses for mediating the transition was the famous series of articles that André Ribaud contributed to the French satirical paper, *Le Canard Enchaîné*, under the title of *La Cour*, with Moisan's brilliant drawings, interpreting the régime of General de Gaulle as if he were Louis XIV. Nowadays the articles are continued under M. Pompidou as *La Régence*. There are some obvious advantages to such a transposition: characters can still on occasions refer to 'the Court', but it is intended in the sense of M. Ribaud; the subversive pamphlet, foisted on Alceste in the same way as one was foisted on Molière by enemies angered by *Tartuffe*, can be readily accepted in a period during which, from 1959 to 1966, no less than 300 convictions were made under a dusty old law which made it a crime to insult the Head of State; above all it has the advantage of anchoring in a more accessible society some of the more far-reaching and complex implications of Alceste's dilemma, personal, social, ethical, political. Once the transition had been made other adjustments had to follow. The sonnet I first wrote for Oronte has now been replaced by something closer to my own experience of today's poetaster. To adapt what John Dryden, one of my masters and mentors in the art of the couplet, said of his great translation of Virgil's *Aeneid*, ' I hope the additions will seem not stuck into Molière, but growing out of him '; no more intrusive, that is, than the sackbut, psaltery, and dulcimer the Jacobean translators of the Bible introduced into the court of Nebuchadnezzar, or the Perigord pies and Tokay that the anonymous translator of 1819 introduces into his version of *Le Misanthrope*. That same version seems to base its Clitandre on Lord Byron. I have used contemporary, but less talented models. The version itself is my form of exegesis.

I was 'educated' to produce jog-trot versions of the classics. Apart from a weekly chunk of Johnson, Pitt the Younger and Lord Macaulay to be done into Ciceronian Latin, we had to turn once living authors into a form of English never spoken by men or women, as if to compensate our poor tongue for the misfortune of not being a dead language. I remember once making a policeman in a Plautus play say something like ' *Move along there* ', only to have it scored through and ' *vacate the thoroughfare* ' put in its place. This tradition lingers in the verse versions of the 19th and 20th centuries. This is a typical piece of ripe Virgilian translation:

Penthesilea furent, the bands leading
Of lune-shield Amazons, mid thousands burns,
Beneath exserted mamma golden zone
Girds warrior, and, a maid dares cope with men.

That would have earned some marginal VGs from my mentors. With the help of Gavin Douglas, John Dryden, Ezra Pound, and Edward Powys Mathers I managed to escape from all this into what I hope is a more creative relationship with foreign tongues. So my translation, when I do it now, is a Jack and the Beanstalk act, braving the somnolent ogre of a British classical education to grab the golden harp.

The problems of the academic coming to grips with a classic of foreign literature, in this case some 3 centuries old, puts me in mind of Francis Galton, the cousin of Charles Darwin, on his travels in Damaraland, Southern Africa in 1851, who wishing to measure the phenomenon of steatopygia in what he called ' a Venus of Hottentots ', but restrained by Victorian *pudeur*, took a series of observations with his sextant, and having obtained the base and angles, proceeded to work out the lady's intriguing ' endowments ' by trigonometry and logarithms. The poet, and the man of the theatre, have to be bolder and more intimate.

The salient feature of Molière's verse is its vigour and energy, rather than any metaphorical density or exuberant invention, and it is this which gives his verse plays their characteristic dramatic pace. In *Le Misanthrope* the effect of the rhyming couplet is like that of a time-bomb ticking away behind the desperation of Alceste, and Célimène's fear of loneliness. The relentless rhythm helps to create the tensions and panics of high comedy, and that *rire dans l' ame* that Donneau de Visé experienced on the first night of the play in 1666. The explosion never comes. But the silence, when the ticking stops, is almost as deafening. There is an almost Chekovian tension between farce and anguish. To create this vertiginous effect verse (and *rhymed* verse) is indispensable. Neither blank verse nor prose will do. I have made use of a couplet similar to the one I used in *The Loiners*, running the lines over, breaking up sentences, sometimes using the odd half-rhyme to subdue the chime, playing off the generally colloquial tone and syntax against the formal structure, letting the occasional couplet leap out as an epigram in moments of devastation or wit. My floating 's is a way of linking the couplet at the joint and speeding up the pace by making the speaker deliver it as almost one line not two. And so on. I have made use of the occasional Drydenian triplet, and, once in Act III, of something I call a ' switchback ' rhyme, a device I derive from the works of George Formby, e.g. in *Mr. Wu*:

Once he sat down – those hot irons he didn't spot 'em

He gave a yell – and cried ' Oh my – I've gone and scorched my . . .
singlet!

or

Oh, Mister Wu at sea he wobbles like a jelly,
but he's got lots of pluck although he's got a yellow . . . jumper!

I have also tried both before and during rehearsals to orchestrate
certain coughs, kisses, sighs and hesitation mechanisms into the
iambic line. These are sometimes indicated by (/) in the text.

An American scholar (forgetting Sarah Bernhardt) said of rhymed
translation that it was ' like a woman undertaking to act Hamlet '. A
similar, though much more appropriate summary of the kinship
between my version and the original was given by my 6 year old son,
Max. ' I know that Molière,' he said, with true Yorkshire chauvinism,
though he was born in Africa, ' she's Jane Eyre's sister.'

Newcastle-upon-Tyne,   TH
January, 1973

Acknowledgements
Many friends have helped with suggestions at various draft
stages. I particularly wish to thank: Rosemarie Harrison; John
Hearsum; Alan Page; and members of the National Theatre
Company.

[vii]

This version of *Le Misanthrope* was first produced by the National Theatre Company at the Old Vic on 22 February 1973 with the following cast:

GILLIAN BARGE	Arsinoé
NICHOLAS CLAY	Acaste
JEREMY CLYDE	Clitandre
PAUL CURRAN	Basque
GAWN GRAINGER	Oronte
JAMES HAYES	Dubois
ALAN MACNAUGHTAN	Philinte
ALEC MCCOWEN	Alceste
CLIVE MERRISON	Secretary of the Academy
DIANA RIGG	Célimène
JEANNE WATTS	Eliante

PRODUCTION	John Dexter
SCENERY AND COSTUMES	Tanya Moisiewitsch
LIGHTING	Andy Philips
MUSIC	Marc Wilkinson
STAGE MANAGER	Diana Boddington
DEPUTY STAGE MANAGER	Tony Walters
ASSISTANT STAGE MANAGERS	Elizabeth Markham Phil Robins
ASSISTANT TO PRODUCER	Harry Lomax

ACT ONE

*(Alceste sits alone in darkness, listening to the music of Lully.
Philinte enters from the party in progress downstairs, switches
on the light, sees Alceste, and turns off the hi-fi.)*

PHILINTE Now what is it? What's wrong?

ALCESTE   O go away!

PHILINTE But what is it? What's wrong?

ALCESTE   Please go away!

PHILINTE Alceste, please tell me what's got into you . . .

ALCESTE I said leave me alone. You spoil the view.

PHILINTE Don't start shouting and, please, hear people out.

ALCESTE No, why should I? And, if I like, I'll shout.

PHILINTE But why this typical ' splenetic fit '?
Though I'm your friend, I don't think friends
                                     permit . . .

ALCESTE Me, your friend? You can cross me off your list.
After what I've just clapped eyes on I insist
our friendship's finished. ' Friends ' (so-called)
                                     who'll sell
their friendship everywhere can go to Hell.

PHILINTE Now that's not fair, Alceste. It's most unjust.

ALCESTE You should be mortified with self disgust.
There's no excuse for it. That sort of trick
revolts all decent men, and makes me sick.
We'd just arrived, and how did you behave?
Downstairs just now, what did I see you do?
You hoist your glass and hail, not hail, *halloo*
some person from a distance, and then zoom
into warm embraces from across the room,
drench the man with kisses, smile and swear
your lasting friendship, shout *mon cher, mon cher*
so many times you sounded quite inspired,
then when you sidled back and I inquired:
Who's that, the long-lost friend you rushed to hug?
all you do's look sheepish, and then shrug.

1

No sooner is his back turned than you start
picking him to pieces, pulling him apart,
all that ' friendship ' faded from your heart.
It's foul and ignominious to betray
your own sincerity in this cheap way.
If, God forbid, it'd been me to blame,
I'd hang myself tomorrow out of shame.

PHILINTE O surely not! I think I'll just remit
your sentence this time, and not swing for it.

ALCESTE Don't think you'll soften me with that sweet smile.
Your humour's like your actions: infantile.

PHILINTE But, seriously, what would you have me do?

ALCESTE Adopt behaviour both sincere and true,
Act like a decent man, and let words fall
only from the heart, or not at all.

PHILINTE But if a man shows friendship when you've met,
you should pay back the compliments you get,
and try as best you can to match his tone
and balance his good wishes with your own.

ALCESTE Disgusting! Every modish socialite
bends backwards to appear polite.
There's nothing I loathe more than empty grins
and cringing grimaces and wagging chins,
politeness mongers, charmers with two faces,
dabblers in nonsensical fine phrases,
outvying one another in their little game
of praise-me-I'll-praise-you. It's all the same
if you're idiot or hero. What's the good
of friendship and respect if it's bestowed
on any nincompoop and simpleton
your praiser-to-the-skies next happens on?
No! No! Not one right-thinking man, not one
'd want such ten-a-penny honours done.
Glittering praise can lose its brilliance
when we see it shared with half of France.
Esteem's based on a scale, it's not much worse
praising nothing than the universe.

2

You'll be no friend of mine if you comply
with these false manners of society.
From the bottom of my heart I must reject
that sort of indiscriminate respect.
If someone honours me I want it known
that it's an honour for myself alone.
Flinging love all over's *not* my line.
The ' buddy ' of Mankind 's no *friend* of mine.

PHILINTE But in society (if we belong that is)
we must conform to its civilities.

ALCESTE No, we must be merciless in our tirade
against this pseudo-civil masquerade.
Let real feelings shine out through our speech,
a deep sincerity where guile can't reach,
not pretty compliments, but true regard,
open, not hidden in some slick charade.

PHILINTE But there're times when speaking out one's mind
'd be ridiculous or plain unkind.
With all due deference to your strict code
there are occasions when restraint is good.
All kinds of social chaos would ensue
if everybody spoke his mind like you.
Supposing there's a man we can't abide,
do we say so, or keep our hate inside?

ALCESTE Say so, say so!

PHILINTE   I see; and would you tell
Emilie, (poor superannuated *belle*,)
she's past all beauty, and a perfect scream
under the make-up and foundation cream?

ALCESTE Yes.

PHILINTE   And Dorilas how much he bores us all
with how-I-won-back-France for Charles de Gaulle,
the Maquis mastermind who saved the war?
Would you say that to him?

ALCESTE   I would, and more!

PHILINTE You're making fun of me.

ALCESTE   *I don't make fun.*

3

In things like this I won't spare anyone.
The City, Politics, the Arts (so called!)
I've seen them all, Philinte, and I'm appalled.
Black rage comes over me, it makes me rave
seeing the dreadful way most men behave.
There's not a walk of life where you don't meet
flattery, injustice, selfishness, deceit.
I'm utterly exasperated and my mind
's made up, I'm finished, finished with mankind!

PHILINTE   Your dark philosophy's too bleak by half.
Your moods of black despair just make me laugh.
I think by now I know you pretty well . . .
we're very like Ariste and Sganarelle,
the brothers in that thing by Molière,
you know, *The School for Husbands,* that one
                                         where . . .

ALCESTE   For God's sake, spare us *Molière* quotations!

PHILINTE   But, please, no more hell-fire denunciations!
The world's not going to change because of you.
Your fond of frankness . . . do you know it's true
that people snigger at this quirk of yours?
Everywhere you go, society guffaws.
Your fulminations on the age's lies
just make you seem comic in most men's eyes.

ALCESTE   So much the better! Comic in their sight?
That only goes to prove that my way's right.
Mankind's so low and loathsome in *my* eyes,
I'd start to panic if it thought me wise.

PHILINTE   I think you'd write off all humanity!

ALCESTE   Because I hate them, all of them, that's why.

PHILINTE   We're living in bad times I know, that's true,
but even so there *must* be just a few . . .

ALCESTE   A few? Not one! Not one a man can trust.
The whole lot fill me with complete disgust.
Some because they're vicious, all the rest
because they nod at vice and aren't depressed
or full of righteous anger at the thought

of wickedness at large, as good men ought.
It's taking tolerance to wild extremes
to tolerate that swine and his low schemes,
that awful, foul, objectionable swine —
the one who's tried to grab this land of mine,
whose trumped-up action's hauled me into court.
Cultivating monsters of that sort!
There's plainly a villain under that veneer.
The truth of what he is is all too clear.
Those sheepish humble looks, that sickly grin
take only those who've never met him in.
The guttersnipe! There's no one who can't guess
the tricks he's stooped to for his quick success.
The niche he's carved himself, in padded plush
makes talent vomit and real virtue blush.
Call him a bastard and everyone hoorays
but he's still the blue-eyed boy of smart *soirées*.
That grinning hypocrite, that nepotist's
on all society reception lists.
Despite his obvious and blatant flaws
his smirk's his Sesame through *salon* doors.
In rat-race intrigue he's a class apart
straight to the post before his betters start.
When I see vice given its head I feel
the pity of it pierce me like cold steel.
In these mood's what I want 's some wild retreat
where humanity and I need never meet.

PHILINTE A little understanding's what's required.
Humanity leaves much to be desired
I know that very well, but let's not rant
about its vices. Let's be tolerant.
Moderation's where true wisdom lies.
What we should be is *reasonably* wise.
You're living in the past. Diogenes
isn't quite the type for times like these.
All your harping on that ancient theme
strikes the modern age as too extreme.

Compromise; accommodate; don't force
your principles to run too stiff a course.
It's sheer, outrageous folly to pretend
you'll change things or imagine you'll amend
Mankind's perversity one little jot.
You think your anger's wisdom, but it's not.
Like you I see a hundred things a day
that could be better, but I don't inveigh
against them angrily, and unlike you,
I've learnt to be tolerant of what men do,
I take them as they come, put up with them.
' Bile ' 's no more philosophical than ' phlegm '.
In social intercourse the golden rule
's not curse, like you, but, like me ' keep
one's cool '.

ALCESTE So, whatever vast disaster or mishap
you're philosophical and never flap?
If you were in my shoes and someone planned
to gain possession of your precious land;
betrayed you, slandered you, what then? What
then?
Would you still show ' tolerance ' for men?
Maligned, betrayed, and robbed! You'd be a fool
to watch all that occur and ' keep your cool '.

PHILINTE But when I see self-interest, graft, deceit,
when I see men swindle, steal, lie, cheat,
I feel about as much sense of dismay
As if I'd seen some beast devour its prey,
or if I'd watched, say, monkeys in the zoo
doing what monkeys are supposed to do.
All your diatribes are off the track.
It's basic human nature you attack.
That's your humanity. There's no escape.
These are the antics of the ' naked ape '.

ALCESTE So, I'm to see myself knocked down, laid low,
and torn to pieces, robbed and never . . . O
it's pointless talking and I'll say no more

6

PHILINTE Calm down, Alceste. And turn your mind to law.
          Your 'hypocrite', remember, and his suit.
ALCESTE   But there's absolutely nothing to dispute.
PHILINTE But you've selected your solicitors?
ALCESTE   Yes, reason and the justice of my cause.
PHILINTE And won't you pay the judge the usual visit?
ALCESTE   No! I see, my case is doubtful is it?
PHILINTE Of course not, no, but if the man's in league
          with others, then there's bound to be intrigue.
ALCESTE   There's right and wrong. There's no two ways
                                                 about it.
PHILINTE Well, I wouldn't be too sure. I rather doubt it.
ALCESTE   I won't budge an inch.
PHILINTE   He will though; he'll plot
          your overthrow.
ALCESTE   And if he does, so what?
PHILINTE You'll find out you were wrong.
ALCESTE   Let's see then, eh?
PHILINTE   But . . .
ALCESTE   I'll gladly see the verdict go his way.
PHILINTE Surely . . .
ALCESTE   My adversary's success
          will only go to show man's wickedness.
          To prove men low enough to prostitute
          fair play, before the world, I'll lose my suit.
PHILINTE What a man!
ALCESTE   That satisfaction 'll be worth
          every penny, though it costs the earth.
PHILINTE Alceste, people'll laugh and call you mad
          to hear you talk like that.
ALCESTE   That's just too bad.
PHILINTE Has the widow you're besotted by eschewed
          frivolity for your stern rectitude,
          this dug-out of ideals? Does Célimène
          share your strenuous moral regimen?
          I'm flabbergasted that, for one whose face
          seems to be turned against the human race,

7

one member of it still can fascinate,
and even more astonished by the one
you've lavished this strange adoration on.
Eliante, whose sincerity commands respect,
who thinks of you most kindly, you reject.
One most respectable Arsinoé,
has feelings for you that are thrown away.
And you love Célimène, whose acid skits
make her the reigning queen of bitchy wits,
a Jezebel, whose whole style typifies
those ' dreadful modern ways ', that you despise.
Faults that in others you ruthlessly attack
in lovely Célimène don't seem so black.
Does beauty cancel them? Or don't you mind?
If you can't *see* her faults you must be blind.

ALCESTE Not blind! No, absolutely wide awake!
No standards lowered for the widow's sake.
Although I love her I'm the first to seize
on all her obvious infirmities.
But not withstanding those, in spite of all,
Le Belle Dame Sans Merci has me in thrall.
The rest is modishness, that's something I,
through my deep love for her, can purify.

PHILINTE That's no mean feat if you're successful. If!
And you're convinced she loves you?

ALCESTE   Positive!
I couldn't love her if she weren't sincere.

PHILINTE Then if her love for you 's so very clear.
why do your rivals cause you such distress?

ALCESTE True love desires uniquely to possess
its object, not go shares with other men.
That's what I've come to say to Célimène.

PHILINTE If I were you her cousin Eliante
'd be the sort of lover that I'd want;
She thinks a lot of you, that's very clear.
She's tender, frank, dependable, sincere.
Sincere, Alceste, which means she's so much more

ALCESTE the sort of person you've a weak spot for.
ALCESTE That's true, and reason tells me so each day.
But love won't function in a rational way.
PHILINTE I'm rather worried though that your affair 's. . . .

(Enter Oronte, glass in hand, from the party downstairs)

ORONTE Lovely party! Marvellous do downstairs!
(to Alceste)
Heard you were up here, though, and thought
what luck
to catch Alceste alone . . . I've read your book.
I know your essays backwards, read the lot!
We two should get acquainted better, what?
You really are a most distinguished man.
I love your work. Consider me your ' fan '.
Your talents draw my homage and applause.
I would so love to be a friend of yours.
Friendship with someone of my stamp and sort
's not to be sneezed at, really, I'd've thought.
Excuse me *(cough)* it's you I've been addressing,
(Alceste looks surprised)
I'm sorry I can see that I'm distressing . . .
ALCESTE No, no, not in the least. It's just I'm dazed
to find myself so eloquently praised.
ORONTE It should be no surprise to hear your name
made much of; why, the whole world does the
same!
ALCESTE Monsieur!
ORONTE Your reputation 's nation-wide.
Not only I, all France is starry-eyed.
ALCESTE Monsieur!
ORONTE In my humble view, for what it's worth,
there's nobody quite like you on God's earth.
ALCESTE Monsieur!
ORONTE Let lightning flash and strike me dead
if there's the slightest lie in all I've said.
To show you let me demonstrate, like this,

and seal all I've been saying with this kiss.
Your hand, then, on our friendship, yours and
mine!

ALCESTE Monsieur!

ORONTE   Not interested? Do you decline?

ALCESTE The honour that you do me 's far too great.
Friendships develop at a slower rate.
It's the very name of friendship you profane
if you repeat the word like a refrain.
It's judgement, choice, consideration pave
the way to friendship and we can't behave
as if we're bosom friends until we've found
we actually share some common ground.
Our characters may prove so different.
we'd soon regret our rushed vows and repent.

ORONTE Excellently put! Your insight and good sense
just make my hero-worship more intense.
If time will make us friends I'll gladly wait,
but, in the meantime, please don't hesitate,
if there's anything at all that I can do,
Elyséewise, a place, an interview,
just say the word. Most people are aware
just what my standing is with those ' up there '.
There can't be many men much more *au fait*
with all that happens at the Elysée.
I'm ' in ' with those that matter, even HE
treats me like his own; yes, honestly!
So count on me to help you ' oil the wheels '.
Now, since you're an author, and a man who feels,
to inaugurate our friendship I'll recite
a little poem I've felt moved to write.
I'd welcome your reactions and some hint
on whether it seems good enough to print.
Perhaps you could suggest (I know it's cheek)
which editors you know are *sympathique*.

ALCESTE I'm afraid I'm not well-suited to the task.

ORONTE O, not well-suited? Why's that may I ask?

10

ALCESTE Frankness is my *forte*. I'm afraid you'd find
I'm uncomfortably prone to speak my mind.

ORONTE Frankness! Just what I ask. No, I insist.
I'm not just looking for a eulogist.
I've come expecting you to be quite straight.
I'll feel resentful if you hesitate.
I'm not afraid of, I demand sincerity.

ALCESTE Since you insist, Monsieur, then yes, I'll try.

ORONTE HOPE . . . it's about a girl, a little thing
who's rather kept me dangling on a string.
HOPE . . . just my inmost feelings, nothing
planned.
It's just as it came out you understand.

ALCESTE Proceed!

ORONTE HOPE . . . what I'd really like to know 's
if the intensity of feeling shows
and if I've got the rhythm right, or wrong.

ALCESTE Read it and we'll see.

ORONTE Didn't take me long.
Not fifteen minutes. Came to me in bed.

ALCESTE Time's immaterial. Please go ahead.

ORONTE HOPE . . . that's the title, HOPE. Before I read . . .

ALCESTE I think we've got the picture. Please proceed!

ORONTE *(reads)*
' Hope was assuaging:
its glimmer
cheered my gloomy pilgrimage
to the gold shrine of your love . . .
a mirage of water pool and palms
to a nomad lost in the Sahara . . .
but in the end it only makes thirst worse '.

PHILINTE That's rather touching. Yes, I like that bit.

ALCESTE *(aside)*
How can you like that stuff, you hypocrite?

ORONTE *(reads)*
' Darling, if this hot trek
to some phantasmal Mecca

of love's consummation
is some sort of Herculean labour
then I've fallen by the wayside.'

PHILINTE Intriguing, yes, I like your turn of phrase.

ALCESTE *(aside)*
Flatterer! It's rubbish, not worth any praise.

ORONTE *(reads)*
' A deeper, darker otherwhere
is unfulfilment . . .

we who have bathed in the lustrous light
of your charisma
now languish in miasmal black despair

and all we hopeless lovers share
the nightmare of the bathosphere.'

PHILINTE That ' dying fall!' It closes beautifully!

ALCESTE *(aside)*
I wish *he'd* fall and break his neck and die
and cart his doggerel with him off to Hell.

PHILINTE I've never before heard verses . . . shaped . . . so
well.

ALCESTE *(aside)*
Good God!

ORONTE *(to Philinte)* It's just your kindness, I'm afraid.

PHILINTE No, no!

ALCESTE *(aside)* What is it then you . . . renegade!

ORONTE *(to Alceste)*
What do *you* think? And don't forget our pact.
Your frank opinion, mind. I don't want tact.

ALCESTE It's very delicate. I think we'd all admit
a need for flattery, at least a bit,
when it's a question of our taste at stake.
We must be careful just what line we take.
I'll tell you something, though. One day I'd read
a certain someone's verses and I said,
' A man in your position *has* to know
exactly to what lengths he ought to go

12

and keep his itch to scribble well in hand.
Poetry's a pastime, understand;
one shouldn't go too far and let the thing
get out of hand and think of publishing.
The man who can't say no and who persists
ends up a sitting duck for satirists.'

ORONTE And just what is it that you're hinting at?
That I waste my time?

ALCESTE   No, I don't say that.
What I told him was . . . I said, ' Now, look,
nothing 's more humdrum than a boring book.
It's the one thing people can't forgive.
They'll always latch onto the negative.
No matter what good qualities you've got,
People'll judge you by your weakest spot.'

ORONTE It *is* my poem that you're getting at!

ALCESTE I wouldn't say that. No! I don't say that.
I reminded him of men in our own times
who'd come to grief through turning out bad
rhymes.

ORONTE Do *I* write badly? Am I one of those men?

ALCESTE I don't say that. This is what I hinted then.
' Why write at all, unless the urge is bad,
and if so, keep it to yourself, don't add
more slim volumes to the mounds of verse.
Writing's mad, but publishing's far worse.
The only poets the public can forgive
're those poor so-and-sos who write to live.
Take my advice, resist the itch, resist
the urge to star on some poor poetry list,
to end up laughing stock and *salon* martyr,
all for some private press's *imprimatur.*'
That's the advice I tried to get across.

ORONTE I take your point, but still I'm at a loss
to know what 's in my poem . . .

ALCESTE   Jesus wept!
It's bloody rubbish, rhythmically inept,

13

vacuous verbiage, wind, gas, guff.
All lovestruck amateurs churn out that stuff.
It's formless, slack, a nauseating sprawl,
and riddled with stale clichés; that's not all.
'Thirst worse' cacophonous, and those 'ek eks'
sound like a bullfrog in the throes of sex.
Ah! terrible stuff gets written nowadays
Our ancestors, though crude in many ways,
had better taste, and, honestly, I'd trade
all modern verse for this old serenade!
     If Good King Harry said to me
     You may possess my gay Paree
     if you will send your love away,
     then this is what I'd say:
     Good King Harry, Sire, thankee
     for offering me your gay Paree,
     I'd liefer keep my love by far,
     yea, Sire, my love, tra-la!
The rhyming's awkward, and the style's *passé*.
but far better than the rubbish of today,
that pretentious gibberish you all admire.
Here speaks the true voice of desire:
     If Good King Harry said to me
     You may possess my gay Paree
     if you will send your love away
     then this is what I'd say:
     Good King Harry, Sire, thankee
     for offering me your gay Paree
     I'd liefer keep my love by far,
     yea, Sire, my love, tra-la!
There speaks the voice of true authentic passion . . .
(Oronte and Philinte laugh)
Mock on, mock on. In spite of current fashion,
I much prefer it to the flowery haze
and gaudy glitter all the critics praise.
ORONTE And I maintain my poem's rather good.
ALCESTE I suppose there's every reason why you should.

You must excuse me if I can't agree.

ORONTE That many others do 's enough for me.

ALCESTE Yes, they can do what I can't, that's pretend.

ORONTE Ah, so you're ' an intellectual ' my friend?

ALCESTE You'd say so, if I praised your verse, no doubt.

ORONTE Your praise is something I can do without.

ALCESTE You'll have to, I'm afraid.

ORONTE   I'd like to read
a poem of your own dashed off at speed.

ALCESTE Mine might be just as bad as yours, God knows,
but I wouldn't shove the thing beneath your nose!

ORONTE Such arrogance! I don't know how you dare . . .

ALCESTE O, go and find your flattery elsewhere!

ORONTE Now, little man, just watch your manners, please.

ALCESTE Don't take that tone with me, you . . . Hercules!

PHILINTE Gentlemen, enough. I beg you, please, no more.

ORONTE Apologise for that behaviour, *or* . . .!

ALCESTE You'll bring your famous ' influence ' to bear?

ORONTE And all I have to do is cross that square.

(Exit Oronte. Philinte watches him go down the stairs and then pours two drinks. He begins to follow Alceste with them.)

PHILINTE You see what your ' sincerity ' can do?
There's bound to be bad blood between you two.
All the man wanted was a little pat.

ALCESTE Don't talk to me.

PHILINTE   But I . . .

ALCESTE   Not after that!

PHILINTE It's too . . .

ALCESTE   Leave me alone.

PHILINTE   If I . . .

ALCESTE   No more, I say.

PHILINTE But what . . .

ALCESTE   *No more.*

PHILINTE   But . . .

ALCESTE   Still?

PHILINTE   Is that the
way . . .?

ALCESTE O, stop following me about, you pest.
PHILINTE I'd better keep my eye on you, Alceste.

(Philinte notices Célimène enter from downstairs. He gives the 2 glasses of champagne to Célimène. Exit Philinte. Célimène approaches the abstracted Alceste, and clinks the glasses together. As Alceste speaks Célimène drains first one glass, then the other.)

ALCESTE I'll come straight to the point if you don't mind.
There're things in your behaviour that I find
quite reprehensible. In fact I'm so annoyed
I honestly can't see how we'll avoid
the inevitable break. I can't pretend –
sooner or later this thing's bound to end.
And if I swore my patience was unending
reality'd soon prove I *was* pretending.

CELIMENE So that's why you stormed off? I see. I see.
Another moral lecture. *(sigh)* Poor me!

ALCESTE It's not a moral lecture. *(pause)* Célimène
you're rather too hospitable to men.
Far too many swarm here round your door.
I'm sorry, I can't stand it any more.

CELIMENE Am I to blame if men can't keep away?
I'm not the one who's leading them astray.
They're sweet. They visit. What do you suggest?
A mounted sentry, or an entrance test?

ALCESTE No, not a sentry, but you might . . . well . . . mm
temper the welcome you extend to them.
I know that there's your beauty, and there's you,
and that's one single entity, not two,
your beauty's something that you can't conceal,
a woman can't sequester sex-appeal –
one glance though from those eyes brings men to
heel.

Then small attentions here, a favour there
keep all your hopefuls from complete despair.
The hopes you dangle out before them all

16

just help to keep them at your beck and call.
If, once or twice perhaps, you could say NO,
they'd take the hint alright, and they'd soon go,
But what I'd like to know 's what freak of luck's
helped to put Clitandre in your good books?
What amazing talents does the ' thing ' possess,
what sublimity of virtue? Let me guess.
I'm at a loss. Now let me see. *I know!*
It's his little finger like a *croissant*, so,
crooked at *Angelina's* where he sips his tea
among the titled queens of ' gay ' Paree!
What makes *him* captivate the social scene?
Second-skin gauchos in crepe-de-chine?
Those golden blow-wave curls (that aren't his
own)?

Those knickerbockers or obsequious tone?
Or is it his giggle and his shrill falsett –
O hoity-toity voice makes him your pet?

CELIMENE You mustn't go on like this. It isn't fair.
Just why I lead him on you're well aware.
You know he's said he'd put in a good word
to get my lawsuit favourably heard.

ALCESTE Lose your lawsuit and have no cause to pander
to odious little pipsqueaks like Clitandre.

CELIMENE It grows and grows this jealousy of yours!

ALCESTE Those you let court you grow, so there's good
cause.

CELIMENE Surely I'd've thought it wouldn't've mattered
to see my friendliness so widely scattered?
You'd really have much more to shout about
if there were only one I'd singled out.

ALCESTE You blame me for my jealousy, but what,
I ask you, sets *me* above that other lot?

CELIMENE The joy of knowing that my love's for you.

ALCESTE Yes, yes, but how can I be sure that's true?

CELIMENE The simple fact I've told you that it's so
should be enough, and all you need to know.

17

ALCESTE But how can I be certain that you're not
saying the same thing to that other lot?
CELIMENE A pretty compliment that is, a fine way
for a lover to be talking, I must say.
To kill all your mad jealousies stone dead
I take back everything that I just said.
Now you won't need to worry any more.
Satisfied?
ALCESTE God, what do I love you for?
If I could only wriggle off the hook,
I'd give thanks to the Lord and bless my luck.
I've done everything I can to break this gaol
and gain my freedom but to no avail.
My efforts just don't get me anywhere.
My love for you's a cross I've got to bear.
CELIMENE It's certainly unique, I must admit.
ALCESTE Nothing in the world compares with it.
Imagination just can't plumb my heart.
The love I bear for you 's a thing apart.
CELIMENE It's the novel way you show it though Alceste.
All you seem to love for 's to protest.
You can't tell crankiness and love apart.
It's bloodymindedness that fires your heart.
ALCESTE Then give my ' bloodymindedness ' some peace
This wilful vacillation's got to cease.
Look, Célimène, there's just the two of us.
Let's use these precious moments to discuss. . . .
(Enter Basque)
BASQUE The marquis 's downstairs, Madame.
CELIMENE Which one?
BASQUE Acaste.
CELIMENE Then show the marquis up, please . . .
ALCESTE Damn and blast!
(Exit Basque)
Can I never have two words with you alone
and must you be ' at home ' to everyone?
CELIMENE I can't not see him. He'd be most upset.

18

ALCESTE I've never known you 'not see' people yet.
CELIMENE But he wouldn't come to see me any more
         if he thought I thought he was a bore.
ALCESTE Would that matter so much, Célimène?
CELIMENE Alceste, we've *got* to cultivate such men.
         They're influential people with a say
         in big decisions at the Elysée.
         Their tongues do nothing much by way of good
         but their sharp edges can and do draw blood.
         Whoever else you may have on your side
         falling foul of that set 's suicide.
ALCESTE What you mean is, given half the chance,
         you'd be at home to all the men in France,
         though all the arguments of reason show . . .

(Enter Basque)

BASQUE The *other* marquis, Ma'am.
ALCESTE *(making as if to leave)*

                              Clitandre! O, no!
CELIMENE And where're you going to?
ALCESTE   I'm off.
CELIMENE   No stay!
ALCESTE Why?
CELIMENE   Please!
ALCESTE   No!
CELIMENE   For me?
ALCESTE   No, I'm away!
         Unless you're really spoiling for a battle
         you'd want to spare me all their tittle-tattle.
CELIMENE Please stay. I want you to.
ALCESTE   I couldn't, no.
CELIMENE O please do what you like, and, go, please, go!

(Enter Eliante and Philinte)

ELIANTE They're coming up the stairs, the two marquis.
         were you aware?
CELIMENE *(nodding, and to Basque)*

                        Champagne and glasses, please.
19

(to Alceste)
Not gone yet?

ALCESTE No, not yet. I'm here to see
you finally decide on them or me.

CELIMENE Ssssshh!

ALCESTE Make up your mind. This very minute!

CELIMENE Such madness!

ALCESTE Yes, but there's some method in it.

CELIMENE Are you demanding I . . .

ALCESTE decide.

CELIMENE Decide?

ALCESTE Decide. My patience has been more than tried.

(Enter Clitandre and Acaste)

CLITANDRE *(still laughing and removing tie)*
We've been at a lateish evening ' over there '.
Hilarious, *(kiss-kiss)* the whole affair!
I was absolutely helpless. Who'd've thought
Elysée functions could provide such sport?
That old buffoon Cléonte convulsed ' the Court '
until the table heaved with stifled laughs
at his gauche manners and his social gaffes.
Couldn't someone let him know that's *not* the way
he'll get ' preferment ' at the Elysée?

CELIMENE That wine-stained tie he wears, those baggy
breeches
have everyone he meets at once in stitches.
He never learns. He just gets more bizarre,
adding new *faux pas* to his repertoire.

ACASTE Talking of weird people, my head's sore
after a session with the world's worst bore,
blabbermouth Damon – on the street, my cab
waiting at the kerbside; blab, blab, blab!

CELIMENE He certainly goes on. He's got the trick
of passing babble off as rhetoric
but all that comes across when Damon speaks
is squeaking gibberish and high-pitched shrieks.

(Clitandre utters a high-pitched shriek)

ELIANTE *(to Philinte)*
What did I tell you. They're off to a good start,
pulling their friends' characters apart.

ACASTE And what about Timante? He's rather odd.

CELIMENE Our cloak-and-dagger-ite! A grudging nod
in passing 's all you get from that tin god.
as though he'd got such urgent things to do
he hadn't a second he could spare for you.
It's all an act. If he's got news, it's PSTs
and sideways glances like stage anarchists.
He'll halt a conversation in mid-word
to whisper something hush-hush, and absurd.
He looks around him, beckons you away,
leans closer, cups his hand, and breathes: *Nice day!*

ACASTE And Géralde?

CELIMENE   Him? O, I've never been so bored!
He'll only deign to mention a milord.
Rank's his mania. His conversations runs
on nothing else but horses, hounds and guns
The Almanach de Gotha, A to Z,
he's learnt by heart and carries in his head.
If anyone's got blood tinged slightly blue
Géralde knows his first name and calls him *tu.*

CLITANDRE He and Bélise are on good terms, I hear.

CELIMENE Poor silly creature, and so dull. My dear
I suffer martyrdoms when she comes round.
Getting conversations off the ground
with her 's like slavery; one sweats and strains
for subjects, honestly one racks one's brains
but she's so unforthcoming, so half-dead,
chat plummets to silence like a lump of lead.
A little warmer? Turned out nice again!
Chilly, don't you think? It looks like rain!
gambits to break the ice with anyone
but not Bélise; one sentence and she's done.
It's bad enough her visiting at all,

21

but dragged out half the day, intolerable.
Look at the clock, yawn, play the busy host,
she no more budges than a wooden post.

ACASTE Adraste?

CELIMENE An utter megalomaniac!
His conversation's just one long attack.
The ' foul Establishment ' 's his constant theme
because it doesn't share his self-esteem.
How could the latest Government 've passed
him over, him, the great-I-am, Acaste?
The ' old-boy network ', ' the incestuous set '
stops him starring in the Cabinet.
Something Machiavellian and underhand
prevents *his* being a power in the land.

CLITANDRE You've heard the trend? These days the rendezvous
for people who are ' in ' 's *chez* you-know-who.

CELIMENE But they only go to Cléon's for the food.

ELIANTE Cléon's cuisine though 's not to be pooh-poohed.

CELIMENE The dinner turns to sawdust on one's lips
when Cléon's served with everything, like chips.
He tells a boring story and you'd swear
the Château Mouton Rothschild 's *ordinaire*.

PHILINTE His uncle Damis though 's well spoken of.

CELIMENE Yes, we're friends.

PHILINTE He's sound and sensible enough.

CELIMENE Yeees! But exasperating nonetheless.
Those superior displays of cleverness!
He's like some sort of robot, stiff and slow,
and programmed only to repeat *bon mots*!
Since he's turned his mind to being a ' wit ',
he's got ' good taste ' and nothing pleases it.
He's supercilious about new plays
The critic is the man who won't show praise;
only idiots laugh, and fools applaud;
the clever thing to be 's blasé and bored.
His weekly condescending book review
's never about the books but his I.Q.

22

ACASTE Yes, dammit, yes, that's Damis to a tee.

CLITANDRE You're marvellous. I love your mimicry.

ALCESTE Go on, go on, and give the knife more twists.
you socialites are such brave satirists
behind men's backs. If one showed up, you'd rush
to greet the man effusively and crush
him to your bosom in a false embrace
and only say *enchanté* to his face.

CLITANDRE Why pick on us, Alceste? You should address
your disapproval to our kind hostess.

ALCESTE No, dammit, no! It's you two that I blame.
Your fawning makes her slander men's good name.
The lady's gifted with malicious wit,
but it's your flattery that fosters it.
Once she finds there's no one to applaud
her badinage she'll soon enough get bored.
Most infringement of the moral code's
the fault of sycophants and fawning toads.

PHILINTE Why take up their cause? You yourself condemn
the frailties we criticize in them.

CELIMENE His whole life-style depends on saying no.
Alceste, agreed? He'd never stoop so low.
No! Mustn't he go on proving he was born
under the stars of dissidence and scorn?
He's not one of us, no, not Alceste;
not wanting to seem so makes him protest.
He's contradictory in every way;
when all the rest are AYES, he's always NAY,
so contradictory he's even peeved
once his own ideas 've been believed.
When someone else has held them he's been known
to demolish opinions that *were* his own.
(Laughter)

ALCESTE They're on your side. You're safe. Go on, enjoy
the public torture of your whipping boy!

PHILINTE But isn't she half-right? It is your way
to contradict whatever people say.

23

No matter what *their* feelings, pro or con,
it's always the opposition that you're on.

ALCESTE Because they're always so far off the track,
I always have good grounds for my attack.
They sometimes flatter and they sometimes sneer,
either shameless and corrupt, or cavalier.

CELIMENE But . . .

ALCESTE   But nothing, though it's the end of me,
I've got to say I hate your repartee.
These people only wrong you when they fawn
on flaws like yours which secretly they scorn.

CLITANDRE Speaking for myself, I really wouldn't know.
I've always found her perfectly just so.

ACASTE The most charming lady that I've ever met.
I haven't noticed any defects yet!

ALCESTE I've noticed plenty, *and* I'm not afraid
of saying so. I call a spade a spade.
If loving someone deeply means you creep,
if love means criticism 's put to sleep,
keep it. That may be love for such as you;
it's not the sort of love that I call true.
I'd banish those wet lovers who kow-towed
to every half-baked thought I spoke aloud,
who laughed at my bad jokes, who cheered my
                                                                        views,
who treated last year's gossip as hot news,
' worshipped the very ground on which I trod '
and grovelled to my whims, as if I'm God.

CELIMENE And if you had your way, my dear Alceste,
we'd say our keenest critics loved us best.
Sweet-talk's finished, kindness (/) no use.
The surest sign of love is foul abuse.

ELIANTE How does that bit in old Lucretius go,
that bit on blinkered lovers? O, you know;
it's something like: ' whatever's negative's
soon metamorphosed by new adjectives:
the girl whose face is pinched and deathly white

24

's not plain anaemic, she's ' pre-Raphaelite.'
The loved one's figures like Venus de Milo's—
even the girl who weighs a 100 kilos!
' Earth Mother ' 's how some doting lover dubs
his monstrous mistress with enormous bubs.
' A touch of tarbrush?' No, that's healthy tan.
The one called ' Junoesque ' 's more like a man.
The slut's ' Bohemian ', the dwarf's virtue
's *multum in parvo* like a good haiku.
There's ' self respect ' for arrogant conceit.
The windbag's extrovert, the dumb's ' discreet ';
stupidity's ' good nature ', slyness ' wit ',
et cetera . . . it's not inapposite!

ALCESTE But *I* . . .

CELIMENE   I think we've heard enough from you.
Come to the balcony and see my view.
(to Acaste and Clitandre)
Going already, gentlemen?

ACASTE   No!

CLITANDRE   No!

ALCESTE *(to Célimène)*
You seem to be worrying in case they go.
(to Acaste and Clitandre)
Go when you like. But let me make this clear.
When you decide to go, I'll still be here.

ACASTE Unless our hostess thinks I'm in the way.
I'm absolutely free.

CLITANDRE   And *I* can stay.

CELIMENE Is this your notion of a joke, Alceste.

ALCESTE I want to see whose presence suits you best.
(Enter Basque)

BASQUE *(to Alceste)*
Sir, there's a man downstairs 'd like a word.
Says its important. Not to be deferred!

ALCESTE There's nothing I'm aware of that can't wait.

BASQUE Something about a ' feud ' to arbitrate.
Perhaps I should say, sir, the person *says*.

he's official, sir. *Academie Française.*
I'd say myself he's *bona fide*, sir:
the car's a black one with a tricolour.

(Enter *Official of the Academie Française*)

ALCESTE They tell me that you're from the *Academ* –

OFFICIAL – *ie Française,* indeed, sir, yes.

ALCESTE   Well, here I am.

OFFICIAL Perhaps a word or two, sir, in your ear?

ALCESTE Then out with it, dear fellow loud and clear.

OFFICIAL The *Academie Française,* whose Members are . . .

ALCESTE At midnight?

OFFICIAL   . . . taking their brandy and cigar
at *Maxim's,* sir, wondered if you've time to spare.
There's a little matter that they'd like to air.

ALCESTE So late?

OFFICIAL   If you don't mind.

ALCESTE   What can they want?

PHILINTE It's that ridiculous business with Oronte.

CELIMENE *(to Philinte)*
What's this?

PHILINTE   O, he was his usual self about
a sonnet of Oronte's and they fell out.
The sort of private row they like to handle.
They don't like media creating scandal.
They simply want to stop it getting worse.

ALCESTE No compromise. I refuse to praise his verse!

PHILINTE Alcèste! It's the *Academicians* though!
I'll come with you. Come on. We'd better go.

ALCESTE If they suppose they're going to persuade . . .
to . . . somehow . . . change my mind, then I'm
afraid,
with all due deference to those gentlemen,
the *Academie Française* can think again.
Admire his poem? No, I'm adamant.
His verse is vile. I can't and won't recant.

26

PHILINTE But couldn't you try to be a little . . .

ALCESTE   No!
It's dreadful and I'll go on saying so.

PHILINTE You ought to be a little more accommodating.
Let's go. We mustn't keep the Members waiting.

ALCESTE I'll go but nothing will induce me to . . .

PHILINTE We must go *now*, Alceste. But couldn't you . . .?

ALCESTE Listen, only a Special Powers Act
passed by the Elysée 'd make me retract,
but, otherwise, whatever Paris thinks,
I'll go on saying that his poem stinks.
The author of that poem should've been
beheaded for it on the Guillotine.
(Laughter)
Dammit, I wasn't aware my words could cause
such wild amusement and inane guffaws.

CELIMENE Go, at once.

ALCESTE   Yes, but I'll be back again
to finish off *our* business, Célimène.

(Exit Alceste. Clitandre and Acaste continue laughing for some moments)

CLITANDRE You're pleased as Punch. You positively beam
with untroubled *joie-de-vivre*, and self-esteem.
But, frankly, do you really have good cause
for this wide-eyed complacency of yours?

ACASTE Well, all things considered, I fail to see
the slightest cause at all for misery.
I'm young and healthy, rich, my blood's as blue
as any in all France can lay claim to.
Connections help, and when your family tree 's
as illustrious as mine it guarantees
an open entrée into most careers:
the Diplomatic Corps, the Grenadiers,
and, if I fancied, my family could fix
some cushy sinecure in politics.
My nonchalant panache, my poise, my flair

27

shine both in *salons* and the open air:
I've ridden, skiied, played polo, fenced
better than any I've been matched against.
I've a lot of talents! And as for wit,
though I say so myself, I've heaps of it.
Impromptu apothegms and suave *bon gout*
got me my column in the right review.
First-night audiences at all new plays
hold back their condemnation or their praise
until they've read ' Acaste's piece,' *then* they know
just what the reactions are they ought to show.
I'm the arbiter. If I'm bored, they're bored,
and if I write SEE THIS the sheep applaud.
Assured and polished and a handsome creature
(my teeth, I think my most outstanding feature)
my sportman's figure and my splendid gear
easily made me *Best Dressed Man* last year.
Where women are concerned I get my way.
I'm *persona grata* at the Elysée.
Comb Europe if you like. You'd be hard put
to find anyone at all so fortunate.
Honestly I couldn't, even if I tried
feel any other way but satisfied.

CLITANDRE The whole world's at your feet. I wonder you
waste time here as often as you do.

ACASTE I wouldn't dream of coming to pay court
in vain; I'm afraid I'm not that sort.
I leave all that for chappies less endowed –
' to burn for beauties pitiless and proud ',
to languish at their feet, and to submit
to haughty treatment. I'll have none of it.
Your half-baked lovers in the end resort
to sighs and blubbing when they're paying court,
and hope to gain, by laying siege with tears,
what merit couldn't in a thousand years.
But pukka men like me, sir, don't fork out
their love on credit and then go without.

All women have their value, men as well
fetch market prices when they want to sell.
If a woman wants to boast she's made a kill
and bagged my heart. All right! She'll foot the bill.
One has to strike a bargain, and to make
the scale weigh even, give and *take*.

CLITANDRE You think you stand a chance the way things go.

ACASTE I've pretty good reasons for believing so.

CLITANDRE I wouldn't be too sure. You've got it wrong.
It's just been wishful thinking all along.

ACASTE That's right, wrong all along, Clitandre.
And to think it's only now the truth has dawned.

CLITANDRE You're sure?

ACASTE No, I've been wrong!

CLITANDRE But can you
prove . . .

ACASTE Wrong, all along!

CLITANDRE Has she confessed her love?

ACASTE No, she treats me badly . . .

CLITANDRE No, really, please!

ACASTE Cold shoulder only.

CLITANDRE Acaste, please don't tease.
What signs *has* she given? Or are there none?

ACASTE None. I'm rejected. You're the lucky one.
She really hates me. Yes, my only hope
's oblivion; poison or a length of rope.

CLITANDRE Nonsense! This quarrelling's no earthly use.
What I suggest we need 's to make a truce.
Then if, for example, I get some sure sign
that Célimène's decided she'll be mine,
or you, I suppose, that she'll be yours,
the one not chosen graciously withdraws,
and lets the favourite take a few lengths lead.

ACASTE Absolutely! A bargain! Yes, agreed!
But sshhh . . .

(Enter Célimène)

CELIMENE Still here?

CLITANDRE   Love roots us to the spot.
ACASTE Was that a car I heard downstairs, or not?
CELIMENE Yes, guess who's turned up now? Arsinoé!
            I had been hoping that she'd stay away.
            The darling's downstairs now with Eliante.
            What's on her mind this time? What can she want?
ACASTE Prim and proper isn't she, Arsinoé?
            Prudish and puritan, or so they say.
CELIMENE It's all hypocrisy. I'm not impressed.
            At heart she's just as randy as the rest.
            All that disdainful holier-than-thou
            hides nothing more holy than a sacred cow.
            She *longs* to get her hooks into a man,
            but, however hard she tries, she never can.
            The sight of others' lovers makes her green
            with jealousy and so ' *the world's obscene* ',
            she says, ' *the age is blind* ' (that's to herself)
            because she knows that she's left on the shelf.
            Her role as puritan's transparent cover
            for her frustrated life without a lover.
            She brands all beauty sinful. She's afraid
            it puts her feeble ' charms ' into the shade.
            She'd like a lover, that's what she'd like best,
            even (can you imagine it?) Alceste!
            If Alceste's nice to me, she's got the nerve
            to think I'm trespassing on *her* preserve.
            She's so envious, poor dear, she takes delight
            in doing me down to others out of spite.
            Prim and proper is she. O that's rich.
            She's stupid, rude . . . in fact a perfect . . . Dar-

(Enter Arsinoé)

            -ling! I was worried for you. Here you are!
            Nice to see you, Arsinoé, my dear!
ARSINOE It's something that I think you ought to hear.
CELIMENE It's good you've come.

(Exeunt Acaste and Clitandre laughing)

ARSINOE   It's just as well they've
                                                              gone.
CELIMENE A drink?
ARSINOE   No, thank you! I've no need of one.
          I've always thought true friendship shows up best
          and puts sincerity to the surest test
          in matters of most importance, such as things
          touching on a friend's good name, which brings
          me here in haste and genuine concern
          to do you and your honour a good turn.
          Yesterday I called on people known
          for their principles and high moral tone
          whose conversation soon came round to you;
          your conduct and the scandals that ensue
          were not thought proper I'm afraid to say:
          the crowds that flock here almost every day
          and you encourage, your flirtatiousness,
          the goings on, found censure in excess
          of what was just (of course, you'll be aware
          whose side I was on in this affair!)
          I did everything I could to justify
          your good intentions and sincerity,
          but, as you well know, even for a friend,
          there are some things one simply can't defend,
          And even I, reluctantly, confessed
          your style of living wasn't of the best.
          People imagine things (you know how it is)
          They see so many ' improprieties '.
          One does hear rumours, dear, but if you chose,
          an effort at reform could soon scotch those.
          Not that I believe you've gone too far,
          God forbid! Well, you know what people are!
          They think the slightest rumour's proof of blame.
          One must be good in deed as well as name.
          I know you'll take this warning as well-meant,
          a token only of my good intent.
          Think about the things I recommend.

Believe me, I speak only as a friend.

CELIMENE Honestly, I'm grateful for your kind concern,
so grateful, let me straightaway return
the favour done me, and, since you've been so nice,
let me offer *you* some good advice.
I'm very grateful, not at all upset,
Honestly, you've put me in your debt.
The friendship that you proved when you related
all this gossip, now must be reciprocated,
In distinguished company the other day
a discussion started on the proper way
for people to live lives of rectitude.
Your name came up at once: *That prude,*
said one, *she's over-zealous, far too keen*
to be the sort of model that I mean.
Pious fraud, said one another *pseud*
plus something unrepeatable and pretty lewd.
Nobody found it in him to excuse
the pompous shambles of your moral views,
that coy blush, that clearly put-on pout
whenever a few bad words get flung about,
that prissy, patently transparent, *moue*
even if the air's turned slightly blue,
that scornful high-horse manner you employ
in all your dealings with the ' hoi polloi ',
your bitter killjoy sermons that resent
everything that's pure and innocent.
One who professes such concern for God
doesn't go to Mass dressed *a la mode!*
(Their words, not mine) and one who seems so
pure
shouldn't spend so much on *haute couture.*
and someone who devotes herself to prayer
reads a Bible, not *Elle* and *Marie Claire.*
She looks like Lady Pious when she prays
but not to the maids she beats and underpays.
She'd daub a fig leaf on a Rubens nude

but with a naked *man* she's not a prude,
I sprang to your defence as best I could,
naturally, but I couldn't do much good.
Denounced their talk as scandal, but no use,
just one good word against so much abuse.
They all ganged up against me. In the end
they came to this conclusion, my dear friend:
Best leave the sins of others well alone
until you've made some headway with your own.
Only a long self-searching can equip
someone to be the age's scourge and whip.
And even then reform's best left to them
ordained by God Almighty to condemn.
' I know *you'll* take this warning as well-meant,
a token only of my good intent.
Think about the things I recommend.
Believe me I speak only as a friend.'

ARSINOE   One lays oneself wide open when one tries,
however constructively, to criticize,
but if this is the reaction that I get,
I can see how deeply that you've been upset.

CELIMENE   No, not at all. It might be a good thing
if everyone took up this ' counselling '.
Frankness may well open people's eyes
to those parts of themselves they fantasize,
their self-deceptions and their vanities.
We ought to make these little talks routine,
a, say, weekly survey of the social scene.
The latest tittle-tattle, all the chat,
the two of us swap gossip, tit for tat?

ARSINOE   Not much gossip about you comes to my ears.
I'm the usual target for their sneers.

CELIMENE   We celebrate, we praise; we scorn, we scold,
and all depending if we're young or old.
When young, we love, then later we abide
by decorum and act all dignified.
And dignity, I gather, 's no bad ploy

when you've got no more youth left to enjoy.
I've heard it helps a woman sublimate
her inability to snare a mate,
and earns her pure frustration a good name.
When I'm your age I may well do the same
and cultivate your scorn of ' turpitude '.
But twenty 's far too soon to be a prude.

ARSINOE A trivial advantage! No cause to shout
and nothing to get so uppity about.
What difference there is gives you no cause
to brag so rudely of this ' youth ' of yours.
But why this tizzy? I'm really at a loss
to know why you flare up and get so cross.

CELIMENE And I, my dear, have no idea why
you should criticize me in society.
It's not my fault, that I should bear the brunt
of all your spinsterish impoverishment.
There's nothing I can do to change the fact
that lovers want me or my looks attract.
I sympathize. But, look, Arsinoé,
the field's wide open. No one's in your way.

ARSINOE As if one cared about your lovers. Pooh!
I don't care what great packs sniff after you.
As if your lovers could make me upset.
Lovers aren't so difficult to get.
If a woman seeks attention, and success,
one knows the price she pays, O, dear me, yes.
Is men's ' pure love ' entirely what it seems?
Is it your ' character ' that fills their dreams?
I doubt it very much. We're all aware
just what you're getting up to everywhere.
There're many women I know well endowed
with all a man could wish, but there's no crowd
of lovers yapping all hours at *their* door.
So what, we ask ourselves, are men here for?
The conclusion that we come to straightaway 's:
Those conquests? Elementary! *She pays.*

34

It's not for your sweet smile that men come here.
Your little victories must cost you dear,
Don't flaunt your petty triumphs out of spite,
or think your looks give you some sort of right
to sneer at others. God, if anyone
were envious of the victories you've won,
she could, by flinging caution to the wind
like you, get lovers, if she had the mind.

CELIMENE Then do! Then do! Ha! Ha! I do believe
you've got some secret weapon up your sleeve.

ARSINOE I think we'd better leave things as they are,
or one of us I'm sure 'll go too far.
Believe me, if I hadn't had to wait,
I'd've gone much sooner, but my driver's late.

CELIMENE You know you're welcome, dear Arsinoé.
Please don't imagine you must dash away.
And, O how very timely, that Alceste's
come back again. I *must* attend my guests.
I'm sure you won't feel sorry if I go.

(Enter Alceste)

I must see what they're doing down below.
Alcèste, dear, entertain Arsinoé,
then she won't think me rude if I don't stay.

ARSINOE So! We're left together for a little chat!
You know, I don't at all object to that.
She couldn't've done better if she'd tried.
I'm overjoyed our visits coincide.
You must realize, Alceste, a woman finds
a lot to love and honour in fine minds.
When I contemplate your gifts, I must confess
I feel immense concern for your success.
But you're neglected and the Powers-that-be
've passed you over, I think, shamefully.

ALCESTE I don't see why the State should condescend
to honour me. What for? I can't pretend
I've rendered any service; so why fret?

35

	There's nothing that I've done they *can* forget.
ARSINOE	Not everybody honoured by the State
	's done something stirring to commemorate.
	Know-how counts, the right time and right place.
	That your talents 're passed over 's a disgrace.
ALCESTE	My talents! Nothing there to shout about.
	I'm very sure that France gets by without.
	You can't expect the Powers-that-be to ferret
	men's buried talents out and dig for merit.
ARSINOE	Real talent doesn't need it. It's with good cause
	that certain people set high store by yours.
	Yesterday I heard your praises sung
	in two high circles of the topmost rung.
ALCESTE	There's so much sheer confusion nowadays,
	everybody gets fair shares of praise.
	It makes the greatest honours seem quite petty
	when they're flung about like cheap confetti.
	Anyone at all! the lowest of the low
	get picture-profiles in *Le Figaro*.
ARSINOE	If only Politics attracted you,
	then your great talents 'd receive their due.
	The slightest glimmerings of interest!
	Just say the word and I could do the rest.
	I've got good friends who'd easily ensure
	you got promotion or a sinecure.
ALCESTE	And what would I do, ME, among such sham.
	I shun such places. It's the way I am.
	Politics! I'm afraid I'm just not suited.
	My lungs can't breathe an air that's so polluted.
	I just don't have the qualities of guile
	to cut a figure there or ' make my pile '.
	The thing I'm best at 's saying what I mean
	not double-talk and-think, and saccharine.
	The man who can't tell lies won't last two ticks
	in the suave chicanery of politics.
	I'm well aware that people who aren't ' in '
	don't get their ribbons and their bits of tin.

What sort of title could ' the Court ' confer
on perfect candour? Mm? *Légion d'Honneur?*
but there are advantages – one needn't grovel
or praise the Minister's most recent novel
or be some *grande dame* 's lap dog, or applaud
the so-called humour of some other fraud.

ARSINOE Well, if you wish, let's leave the matter there.
What worries me far more though 's your affair.
Quite frankly and sincerely I'd prefer
your heart bestowed on anyone but *her*.
You deserve far better, someone far above
the creature you've entrusted with your love.

ALCESTE Think of what you're saying. You pretend
to be the woman that you slander 's friend . . .

ARSINOE I know, but I feel affronted, hurt, and sad,
to see the sufferings your poor heart 's had.
I feel for you, my friend, but I'm afraid
I have to tell you that your trust's betrayed.

ALCESTE Thank you! I appreciate your kind concern.
It's things like that a lover wants to learn!

ARSINOE My friend she may be, but I've got to say
a fine man like yourself 's just thrown away
on one like Célimène whose love's all show.

ALCESTE You may be right. I really wouldn't know
what goes on in people's hearts. But it's unkind
to put suspicious thoughts into my mind.

ARSINOE Of course, if you're quite happy to remain
deceived, there's nothing simpler. I'll refrain.

ALCESTE No, but innuendoes I can do without.
There's nothing more tormenting than half-doubt.
And I'd be far more grateful if you tried
to tell me facts that could be verified.

ARSINOE Very well, that's good enough for me!
I'll give you evidence that you can *see*.
Come with me to my house and there I'll give,
once and for all, I hope, proof positive
of the infidelities of Célimène.

Then, if you ever feel like love again,
if may be that Arsinoé can find
some far gentler way of being kind.

(Exeunt Alceste and Arsinoé)

ARSINOE: It's not for your sweet smile that men come here.
                    Your little victories must cost you dear.   *(Act I, p. 35)*

CELIMENE (Diana Rigg)   ARSINOE (Gillian Barge)

PHILINTE: In social intercourse the golden rule
's not curse, like you, but, like me, 'keep one's cool'.
(Act I, p. 6)

ALCESTE (Alec McCowen)   PHILINTE (Alan MacNaughton)

ALCESTE: Then give my 'bloodymindedness' some peace.
          This wilful vacillation's got to cease.   (Act I, p. 18)

ALCESTE (Alec McCowen)   CELIMENE (Diana Rigg)

CELIMENE: He looks around him, beckons you away, leans closer, cups his hand, and breathes: *Nice day!*   (*Act I, p. 21*)

CLOTANDRE (Jeremy Clyde) ALCESTE (Alec McCowen)
CELIMENE (Diana Rigg) ACASTE (Nicholas Clay)

CELIMENE: When someone else has held them he's been known
to demolish opinions that *were* his own. (*Act I, p. 23*)

l. to r. ELIANTE (Jeanne Watts) PHILINTE (Alan MacNaughton)
ALCESTE (Alec McCowen) CLITANDRE (Jeremy Clyde) CELIMENE
(Diana Rigg) ACASTE (Nicholas Clay)

ACT TWO

ELIANTE, PHILINTE.

PHILINTE Never in my life, never have I met
a man so stubborn and so obstinate.
We thought we'd have all night to stand about
before this weird affair got sorted out.
Academicians can't have ever heard
another case so trivial and absurd;
tried everything they knew to budge Alceste,
but, at each attempt to shift him, he'd protest:
No, gentlemen, he says, No, absolutely not!
I won't take back a thing. No, not one jot.
What is it that he wants my praises for?
Recommendation for the Prix Goncourt?
It's no dishonour that he can't write well.
One can be bad and still respectable.
A man of distinction in every way,
brave and brilliant, but not Corneille!
His style of living's lavish, and, of course,
he looks magnificent astride a horse;
he's marvellous in many, many ways –
I'll praise his grand munificence, I'll praise
his expert fencing and his spry ' gavotte '
but his poetry, no, absolutely not.
That sort of doggerel, slapdash and slipshod.
's best read aloud – before a firing squad!
After fresh persuasions and more parley
the Members brought him to a grudged finale,
and almost had to go down on their knees!
This was his concession: *I'm hard to please.*
I'm sorry I'm so grudging with my praise

43

(Collapse of stout Academie Française!)
Believe me, he went on, *how very sad*
it makes me here *to say your sonnet's bad!*
On that the two shook hands. M. Malraux
seemed heartily relieved to see him go.

ELIANTE   He is a *bit* obsessive, I suppose.
but my admiration for him grows and grows.
It's heroic, even noble, how he clings
to his proud motto: *Frankness in all things.*
These days that sort of virtue 's very rare.
There should be people like him everywhere.

PHILINTE   The more I know of him the more bizarre
it seems to me his slavish passions are.
Given the kind of star Alceste's born under,
the fact he loves at all 's an earthly wonder.
I'm utterly amazed, but far, far more
that it's your cousin he 's a weak spot for.

ELIANTE   Clearly a case of ' Unlike poles attract '.
They haven't much in common, that's a fact.

PHILINTE   From what you've seen, do you believe she cares?

ELIANTE   It's so difficult to say in these affairs.
How *can* one tell, Philinte. I think you'd find
she was confused as well in her own mind.
Sometimes she loves and doesn't quite know why.
Sometimes she swears she does, but it's a lie.

PHILINTE   I rather think our friend 's in for far more
from your dear cousin that he 's bargained for.
If I were him I'd turn my thoughts elsewhere
and put my feelings in *your* tender care.

ELIANTE   I can't disguise I care and wouldn't try.
It's things like this demand sincerity.
Although it's not to me his feelings turn
his welfare and not mine 's my one concern.
For his sake I'd be only too delighted
if, in the end, our two friends *were* united,
but if it comes about (and it might well,
love always being unpredicable)

	things don't work out exactly as he's planned
	and Célimène gives someone else her hand,
	then I'll be waiting to accept Alceste
	and not be bothered that I'm second best.
PHILINTE	And how could I object when I approve
	the focus of your interests and love?
	Alceste can bear me out on how I've tried
	to speak on your behalf and take your side.
	But if and when they marry, *if* and *when*
	Alceste at last succeeds with Célimène,
	and you must put your feelings on the shelf,
	I'll gladly, gladly offer you myself.
	I'd feel most honoured, absolutely blessed
	to offer you my love as second best.
ELIANTE	Ah, Philinte, you're making fun of me!
PHILINTE	No, I'm sincere. I mean it. Seriously.
	If this were the occasion, Eliante, I'd lay
	my heart wide open; and so I will; one day.

(Enter Alceste)

ALCESTE *(to Eliante)*
Help me punish her! This is the last straw.
My constancy can't stand it any more.

ELIANTE But what is it?

ALCESTE   I just don't want to live.
I'll kill myself. There's no alternative.
The world could hurtle back to Nothingness
and I'd be stoical. But this! But this!
It's all . . . my love's . . . I can't speak even . . .
                                                    I . . .

ELIANTE Now come, Alceste. You must calm down. Please
                                                    try.

ALCESTE God in Heaven. How can one reconcile.
something so beautiful and yet so vile.

ELIANTE But what's happened?

ALCESTE   Over! Done! Who'd've
                                          believed . . .?

She . . . it's Célimène . . . she's . . . *I've been*
deceived!

ELIANTE Are you sure?

PHILINTE   Jealousy creates all kinds
of fantastic monsters in suspicious minds.

ALCESTE Go away, you! The letter I've got here
in her own writing makes it all too clear.
A letter to . . . Oronte! This envelope
contains her blackened name, my blasted hope.
Oronte! Of all the men *the* unlikeliest!
He wasn't even *on* my rivals' list.

PHILINTE Letters can be deceptive and the harm
one imagines done a false alarm.

ALCESTE I've told you once before. Leave me alone.
Bother yourself with problems of your own.

ELIANTE Now, now, you must keep calm and this
                                                    disgrace . . .

ALCESTE is something only you can help me face.
It's to you now that I turn to set me free
from this bitter, all-consuming agony.
Avenge me on your cousin, who betrays
a tenderness kept burning all these days.
Avenge me, Eliante, I'm torn apart.

ELIANTE Avenge you? How can I?

ALCESTE   Accept my heart.
Take it, instead of the one who tortures me.
Yes, take it, please. It's simple, don't you see
By offering you my tenderest emotion,
my care, attention and profound devotion,
by laying all my feelings at your feet,
I can get my own back on her foul deceit.

ELIANTE As sorry as I am to see you suffer
and not ungrateful for the love you offer,
I can't help wondering when you decide
that everything's been over-magnified
and you've found out you've made too big a fuss,
what happens to your vengeance? And to us?

46

Lovers' quarrels see-saw, we all know,
backwards and forwards, up/down, to and fro,
bad reports believed, then unbelieved,
sentenced one minute, and the next reprieved.
Even when it's clear, the case quite watertight,
guilt soon becomes innocence, wrong right.
All lovers' tiffs blow over pretty soon,
hated this morning, loved this afternoon.

ALCESTE No! The knife's been twisted too far in.
I'm absolutely through with Célimène!
Ab-so-lute-ly! No question of retreat.
I'd rather die than grovel at her feet.
Is that her now? It is. I feel my hate
go fizzing up its fuse to detonate!
I'll spring the charge on her. She'll be non-plussed.
Then when I've ground her down into the dust,
I'll bring to you a heart made whole again
and free of the treacherous charms of Célimène.

(Enter Célimène)

God, help me master my emotion!
CELIMENE Ah!
(to Alceste) Now, Alceste, what's all this new
                                             commotion?
What on earth's the meaning of those sighs,
those terrible black looks, those blazing eyes?
ALCESTE Of all foul things on Earth I know of few
whose damnable evil 's a patch on you.
If Heaven or Hell, or both combined
spawned worse demons, they'd be hard to find.
CELIMENE Charming! Thank you! Now that's what I call
                                             love.
ALCESTE It's no laughing matter. I've got proof
of your deceptions. Incontestable! Now
you should blush, not laugh, if you know how
All my premonitions have proved right.
It wasn't for nothing that my love took fright.

47

You see. You see. Suspicion 's a good scout.
I followed in its trail and found you out.
In spite of your deceit my guiding star
's led me to discover what you are.
Love's something no one has much power over.
It's growth's spontaneous in every lover
Force is quite useless. Hearts can't be coerced
except if they consent to submit first,
and if, at the very outset, Célimène,
you'd rejected my advances, there and then,
I'd've only had my luck not you to blame,
but to have been encouraged and had the flame
fanned into hopeful fire so shamelessly
's unforgiveable; sheer downright treachery!
And I've got every reason to complain
and every reason now to give full rein
to anger, yes, after such hard blows,
watch out, Célimène, be on your toes,
I'm not responsible for what I do.
My anger 's on the prowl because of you.

CELIMENE   Such wild behaviour! *(to Philinte)* Too much wine
                                            downstairs?

ALCESTE   No, too much Célimène and her affairs.
The baited barb of beauty. Gobble that,
you're hooked, you're skinned, you're sizzling in
                                       the fat.

(Pause)

Looks are so deceptive. I thought you *must*
've meant sincerity and truth and trust.

CELIMENE   What is it then that's given you offence?

ALCESTE   How very clever! You! All innocence!
Very well then, Straight down to the cause.
Look at this. *(produces letter)* This writing? Is it
                                       yours?
Of course! This letter damns you right enough.
There's no plea possible against such proof.

CELIMENE   And is it *this*, that all your upset 's for?

48

ALCESTE	Look at it, Célimène, and blush some more.
CELIMENE	Why should I blush?
ALCESTE	Brazen as well as sly!
	There's no signature and so you'll lie.
CELIMENE	Why should I disown it when it's mine?
ALCESTE	Read it! You're condemned by every line.
	Look, and deny you're guilty if you can.
CELIMENE	Really, you're a foolish, foolish man.
ALCESTE	No shrugging off this letter, I'm afraid,
	and is it any wonder I'm dismayed
	that it's Oronte's love that you really want.
CELIMENE	Who told you that this letter's to Oronte?
ALCESTE	Those who gave me it. Perhaps there's some mistake?
	And if there is, what difference does it make?
	Am I less injured, you less stained with shame?
CELIMENE	But if it's to a woman, where's the blame?
	Can you interpret *that* as an affront?
ALCESTE	Ah, very clever! Absolutely brilliant!
	So that's the way you'll throw me off the scent?
	Oh, of course, that finishes the argument.
	How dare you try on such deceitful tricks?
	Or do you take us all for lunatics?
	So now let's see what deviousness you try
	to give support to such a blatant lie.
	A woman! How can you possibly pretend
	this note's intended for a woman friend?
	Please explain, to clear yourself, just what
	does this mean here . . .
CELIMENE	I certainly will not!
	Your behaviour really puts me in a fury.
	What right have you to play at judge and jury?
	How dare you say such things? It's a disgrace
	to fling such accusations in my face.
ALCESTE	Now let's not lose our tempers or complain.
	This expression here now. Please explain . . .
CELIMENE	No! No! I'll do nothing of the kind.

	I don't care anymore what's on your mind.
ALCESTE	Please explain what proves this letter to be **meant**
	for a woman friend, then I'll relent.
CELIMENE	No, I'd rather you believed it's to Oronte.
	It's *his* attentions that I really want.
	His conversation, his ' person ' pleases me.
	So say anything you like and I'll agree.
	Carry on your quarrel as you think best,
	but don't, don't question *me* again, Alceste.
ALCESTE	God, could anything more cruel be invented,
	and was ever any heart so much tormented?
	I come to complain how cruelly I'm used
	and in the end it's me who stands accused!
	The woman does her damndest to provoke
	my jealousy then treats it as a joke,
	lets me believe the worst, then crows, and cackles,
	and I can't hack away these dreadful shackles,
	the heavy ball and chain, the dangling noose,
	I see them very well but can't break loose.
	O what I need to steel me 's cold disdain
	to scorn ingratitude and sneer at pain.
	(to Célimène)
	Ah, you're diabolical! You take a man's weak spots
	and tie the poor fool up in subtle knots.
	Please clear yourself, it's more than I can bear
	to leave the question hanging in the air.
	Please don't make me think you love another man.
	Show me this note's innocent, if you can.
	Try to *pretend* you're faithful. Please, please, try.
	And I'll try to pretend it's not a lie.
CELIMENE	Jealousy 's turned your brain, my poor friend.
	You don't deserve my love. Pretend? Pretend?
	Why should I lower myself to be untrue
	I'd like to be informed? To humour you?
	Well, really! And if I had another *beau*,
	wouldn't I be sincere and tell you so?

50

Are all my frank assurances in vain
against those fantasies you entertain?
Should they matter? You've had my guarantee.
Even to half-believe them insults me.
A woman who confesses love like this
breaks through great barriers of prejudice.
The so-called ' honour of the sex ' prevents
a frank expression of her sentiments.
If a woman's overcome that sense of shame
and the man's not satisfied, then *he's* to blame.
After all the woman's had to struggle through
surely the man could be assured it's true.
Ah! Your suspicions make me angry. You're . . .
you're absolutely not worth caring for.
It's too absurd. I'm really not quite sane
to go on being kind when you complain.
I should find someone else instead of you.
Then all your allegations *would* come true.

ALCESTE   Ah, it never fails to take me by surprise,
my feebleness. Your sweet talk may be lies,
but I must learn to swallow it all whole.
I'm at your faithless mercy, heart and soul.
I'll hang on till the bitter end and see
just how far you'll go with perfidy.

CELIMENE   No, you don't love me as you really ought.

ALCESTE   My love goes far beyond the common sort.
So keen was I to show it that I wished
you were unloveable, impoverished,
a pauper, and a beggar, and low-born,
the object of derision and of scorn
and with one act of sudden transformation
my love could raise you from your lowly station,
in one fell swoop make up for that poor start,
by making a public offer of my heart,
so that the world could see and know and say:
He made her everything she is today.

51

CELIMENE O such benevolence deserves a plaque!
          Whatever could I do to pay you back . . .
          O here's Dubois. About to emigrate!

(Enter Dubois laden with luggage)

ALCESTE What's this?

DUBOIS   Allow me, sir, to explicate.

ALCESTE Please do.

DUBOIS   It's something most bizarre. Mysterious.

ALCESTE But what?

DUBOIS   Yes, very strange, and *could* be serious.

ALCESTE But how?

DUBOIS   Have I your leave to . . .

ALCESTE   speak, or shout
          for all I care, but, quickly, spit it out.

DUBOIS In front of . . .

ALCESTE   all the world if needs be, man.
          For God's sake tell me, clearly, *if* you can.
          And *now*.

DUBOIS   The time, sir, 's come to expedite,
          to put it rather crudely, sir, our flight.

ALCESTE Our what?

DUBOIS   Our flight, sir, flight. We must proceed
          with all due caution, but at double speed.

ALCESTE What for, man?

DUBOIS   Sir, once more let me stress
          we must leave Paris by the next express.

ALCESTE Leave Paris, why?

DUBOIS   No time at all to lose.
          No time for long farewells or fond adieus.

ALCESTE *What does this mean?*

DUBOIS   It means (to specify,
          to be absolutely blunt) it means . . . Goodbye!

ALCESTE I'm warning you, Dubois . . . Dubois, look here.
          Start again, at once, and make things clear.

DUBOIS A person, sir; black looks, black coat, black hat,
          appeared, sir, in the kitchen, just like that,

deposited a paper, and then went –
a very legal-looking document.
It looks to me a little like a writ
with stamps and signatures all over it,
some sort of summons, surely, but I'm blessed
if I could make it out, Monsieur Alceste,

ALCESTE And why, please, does this paper that you say
the man delivered mean our getaway.

DUBOIS Then after, sir, about an hour or so,
another person called, and *him* you know,
he calls quite often on you, seemed distressed
to find you out tonight, Monsieur Alceste,
yes, most disturbed, but knowing he could send
dependable Dubois to help his friend,
he urged me, very gravely, to convey,
without procrastination or delay,
this urgent message to my master, sir . . .
his name was . . . just a minute . . . mm . . .
                                        mm . . . er . . .

ALCESTE O never mind his name. What did he say?

DUBOIS One of your friends, he was, sir, anyway.
He said, and I repeat, sir: *Tell Alceste*
he must leave Paris and escape arrest.

ALCESTE Escape arrest, and was that all he said?

DUBOIS Except it would be better if you fled.
He dashed a quick note off for me to bring.
He said the note would tell you everything.

ALCESTE Give it to me then.

CELIMENE   What's all this about?

ALCESTE I'm not quite sure. I'm *trying* to find out.
(to Dubois)
You, you great idiot, not found it yet?

DUBOIS *(after a long search)*
I must have left it somewhere . . . I forget . . .

ALCESTE I don't know what . . .

CELIMENE   Alceste! You ough to sort
this nonsense out at once, you really ought!

ALCESTE   No matter what I do, it seems that fate
          's imposed its veto on our *tête-à-tête*.
          I've still got many things to say to you.
          When I come back, please, one more interview?

ALCESTE: How very clever! You! All innocence!   (*Act II, p. 48*)

CELIMENE (Diana Rigg)   ALCESTE (Alec McCowen)
ELIANTE (Jeanne Watts)

DUBOIS: *We must leave Paris by the next express.*   (*Act II, p. 52*)

ALCESTE (Alec McCowen)   DUBOIS (James Hayes)
CELIMENE (Diana Rigg)

ACT THREE

ALCESTE, PHILINTE

ALCESTE No, my mind's made up I've got to go.
PHILINTE Must you? Really? However hard the blow.
ALCESTE Coax and wheedle to your heart's content.
My mind's made up, and what I said I meant.
This age is fastened in corruption's claws.
I'm opting out of this foul world of yours.
this world where wrong seems right, and right
                                    seems wrong
can count me out of it. I don't belong.
After what's happened in my lawsuit, how . . .
how can I possibly remain here now?
Everything that renders life worthwhile,
everything that counters lies and guile –
Justice, Honour, Goodness, Truth and Law
should've crushed that swine, or else what's
                                    Justice for?
All the papers said my cause was just
and I'm the one who's trampled in the dust.
Thanks to black perjury that ruthless sinner
whose past's notorious comes off the winner.
Truth drops a curtsey to the man's deceit,
and Justice flops, and crawls to kiss his feet!
He'd get away with anything; he'd quote
some legal precedent, then cut my throat.
His hypocritical grimace never fails –
one quick smirk at the jury tips the scales.
To crown it all the Court gives him a writ.
Harried and hounded by that hypocrite!
Not satisfied with that. Not satisfied,
there's yet another trick the devil's tried.

A pamphlet's just been published, and suppressed.
All booksellers that stock it risk arrest.
This obscene libel seeks to implicate
some of the closest to the Head of State.
Although he hasn't mentioned me by name,
he's dropped hints to the Press that I'm to blame.
and, look at this, this headline here, just look!
SEARCH FOR AUTHOR OF SUBVERSIVE BOOK:
EXPERT OPINION ANALYSES STYLE!
And a picture of Oronte (just *see* that smile!)
Which author does ' expert ' Oronte suggest:
' There's only one it could be, that's Alceste.'
Oronte! Someone I tried my very best
to be quite fair with, yes, Oronte, the pest,
coming with his verses for a ' fair ' critique,
and when I *am* fair, and, in all conscience, seek
to do justice to the truth and him as well,
he helps to brand me as a criminal.
All this irreconcilable bad blood
and all because his poem was no good!
And if that's human nature God forbid!
If that's what men are like then I'm well rid.
This is the sort of good faith, self respect,
concern for truth, and justice I expect.
Their persecution 's more than I can face.
Now I'm quitting this benighted place,
this terrible jungle where men eat men.
Traitors! You'll never see my face again.

PHILINTE   I'm pretty sure the problem's not as great
as you make out. If I were you I'd wait.
Whatever charges they've trumped up, Alceste,
you've managed so far to avoid arrest.
Lies can boomerang and choke the liar.
All these tales and scandals could backfire.

ALCESTE   He doesn't mind. He thrives on his disgrace.
His crimes seem licensed. Far from losing face
his stock 's sky-high; he's lionised in town,

and all because he's made me look a clown.
PHILINTE Up till now most people have ignored
the malicious gossip that he's spread abroad,
and so I wouldn't worry any more
if I were you; at least not on that score.
As for your lawsuit, where you rightly feel
hard done by, you could easily appeal.
ALCESTE No second hearings! I accept the first.
The last thing that I'd want is it reversed.
Let it stand. Then posterity 'll know
how far corruption and abuse can go.
proof of all the mean and dirty tricks
of Mankind circa 1966.
If it costs 20,000 francs, I'll pay;
I'll pay, and earn the right to have my say,
denounce the age and hate man and dissever
myself from all his wickedness for ever.
PHILINTE But after all . . .
ALCESTE   But after all! What, what
do you propose to say about all that
that 's not superfluous. You wouldn't dare
try to excuse this sickening affair.
PHILINTE No! No! Everything you say. Agreed! Agreed!
The world *is* governed by intrigue and greed.
Cunning and fraudulence *do* come off best,
men *ought* to be different, yes, Alceste,
but does man's lack of justice give you cause
to flee society with all its flaws.
It's through these very flaws we exercise
the discipline of our philosophies.
It's virtue 's noblest enterprise, the aim
of everything we do in virtue's name.
Supposing probity *were* general,
hearts were open, just and tractable,
what use would all our virtues be, whose point,
when all the world seems really out of joint,
's to bear with other 's contumely and spite,

	without annoyance, even though we're right.
	Virtue in a heart can counteract . . .
ALCESTE	Quite a performance that, yes, quite an act!
	You've always got so many things to say;
	Philinte, your fine talk's simply thrown away.
	What reason tells me I already know:
	it's for my good entirely if I go.
	I can't control my tongue. It won't obey.
	I'm not responsible for what I say.
	Look at all the trouble I've incurred!
	Trouble seems to stalk my every word.
	Now, leave me to wait here. And no more fuss!
	I've a little proposition to discuss
	with Célimène and what I mean to do
	's find out what her love is: false or true.
PHILINTE	Let's go up to Eliante. We could wait there.
ALCESTE	I've too much on my mind I must prepare.
	You go. I'm better left to nurse this mood
	of black resentment here in solitude.
	This gloomy little corner suits me best.
	(sits)
	The perfect setting! O I'm so depressed.
PHILINTE	You'll find yourself bad company in that state.
	I'll fetch down Eliante to help you wait.

(Exit Philinte. Enter Célimène and Oronte)

ORONTE	I need some proof. It goes against the books
	to keep a lover years on tenterhooks.
	If you welcome my attentions, as you say,
	please stop wavering and name the day.
	Some little gesture that would help to prove
	that you reciprocate my ardent love.
	And all I ask 's Alceste's head on a plate.
	Banish him today and don't prevaricate.
	Please say to him . . . today . . . please . . .

Célimène,
say: *Never show your face round here again!*

60

CELIMENE What's happened between you two, I'd like to
know?
You thought him marvellous not long ago.
ORONTE The whys and wherefores just don't signify.
More to the point though 's where your feelings lie.
Keep one of us and set the other free.
You really have to choose: Alceste or me.
ALCESTE *(emerging from his corner)*
Choose, yes, choose. Your friend here 's justified
in his demands which I endorse. Decide!
His impatience is my own, his anguish mine.
I too insist on having some sure sign.
Things can't go on like this indefinitely.
The time has come to chose: Oronte or me!
ORONTE I've no desire to prejudice your chances
by indiscreet, importunate advances.
ALCESTE Jealousy or not, I certainly don't want
to share her heart with you, Monsieur Oronte.
ORONTE And if she chooses your love and not mine . . .
ALCESTE If it's to *you* her sympathies incline . . .
ORONTE I'll give up all those hopes I had before . . .
ALCESTE I swear I'll never see her any more.
ORONTE Now, you can speak. No need to hum and hah.
ALCESTE Don't be afraid to tell us how things are.
ORONTE Only decide which one 's the one for you.
ALCESTE To clinch the matter, choose between us two.
(Pause)
ORONTE It can't be difficult to pick one out!
ALCESTE Can you hesitate at all, or be in doubt?
CELIMENE This isn't the time and place and that's a fact.
O such demands. Please, gentlemen, some tact!
It's not that I've got anything to hide,
my heart's not wavering from side to side,
but what I *do* find difficult to do
's announce my choice in front of both of you.
I think that anything at all unpleasant
shouldn't be spoken with another present.

It's possible to hint one's attitude
without going to extremes and being rude.
I think that gentle clues are quite enough
to let a lover know he's lost his love.

ORONTE No, not at all. It's frankness that we want.
I've no objections.

ALCESTE   And I'm adamant.
I insist. Choose now between our loves.
I surely don't need handling with kid-gloves.
You try to keep the whole world on a string.
It's got to end at once, this wavering.
No more half-hints, no titillating clues,
We want it cut and dried: accept/refuse.
Silence itself 's a sort of answer though.
I take it silence means quite simply: NO!

ORONTE I'm grateful that you've been so down-to-earth.
I second what you say for all I'm worth.

CELIMENE I'm really quite fed up of this affair.
Demanding this and that! It isn't fair.
Haven't I told you why I hesitate?
Here's Eliante. Ask her. She'll arbitrate.

(Enter Eliante and Philinte)

Eliante! Look, I'm the victim of a plot.
They cooked it up together, like as not.
They both go on and on to make me choose,
which one of them I'll have, and which refuse
They want me to announce it just like that,
one to be chosen, one to be squashed flat.
Please tell them, Eliante, it's just not done.

ELIANTE If you want allies, sorry. *I'm* not one.
I belong to the opposition. I'm inclined
to side with people who can speak their mind.

ORONTE *(to Célimène)*
It's pointless you're protesting I'm afraid.

ALCESTE You can't depend on Eliante for aid.

ORONTE Please speak, and put an end to our suspense.

ALCESTE Or don't. It doesn't make much difference.
ORONTE One little word; then let the curtain fall.
ALCESTE I'll understand if you don't speak at all.

(Enter Arsinoé, Acaste, Clitandre)

ACASTE *(to Célimène)*
Have you two minutes you can spare for us?
We've got a ' little something ' to discuss.
CLITANDRE *(to Alceste and Oronte)*
A good thing you're here too. The reason why
you'll discover to your horror by and by.
ARSINOE Forgive me for intruding once again,
but they requested it, these gentlemen,
who turned up at my house in such a state
of agitation to insinuate
such dreadful things against you, dear, that . . .
well . . .
they seemed quite utterly incredible.
Of course I couldn't believe that it was you,
knowing how kind you are; and thoughtful too.
I said: *No, it can't be!* The case they made
did seem rather damning, I'm afraid.
Forgetting, then, our little *contretemps*
for ' auld lang syne ', my dear, I've come along
with these two gentlemen to hear you clear
yourself at once from this new slander . . . dear.
ACASTE Yes, let's all be calm and civilized and and see
just how you bluff this out and wriggle free.
This is a letter to Clitandre from you.
CLITANDRE And this is to Acaste, this *billet doux.*
ACASTE We won't need any expert to decypher
this all too well-known hand we've all an eye for.
I've had, and so, I know, have all of you,
sizeable amounts of *billet doux,*
so proof's superfluous. This little note
's a fine example, gentlemen. I quote:
(reads)

63

My dear Clitandre

' What a strange man you are to moan when I'm in high spirits and to complain that I'm never so lively as when I'm not with you. Nothing could be further from the truth. And if you don't come very soon to be my pardon for this insult, I'll never forgive you as long as I live. That great hulk of a Viscount. *(He ought to have been here!)* . . . That great hulk of a Viscount, you complain of first, isn't my type at all. Ever since I watched him spitting for at least three quarters of an hour into a well to make circles in the water, I've not much cared for him. As for the little Marquis *(that's me, gentlemen, though I shouldn't boast)* . . . As for the little Marquis, who held my hand so interminably yesterday, he's of no account at all, absolutely insignificant, a tailor's dummy, that's all the little Marquis is. As for that character in green velvet *(your turn, Alceste)* . . . As for that character in green velvet well, he's occasionally amusing with his blunt irascibility and forthright ways, but there are a million other times when I find him the world's worst bore. As for the would-be poet *(your bit this)* . . . as for the would-be poet, who fancies himself one of the intelligentsia, and tries desperately to pass himself off as an author, in spite of what everybody tells him, I can't even be bothered listening any more, and his prose is about as tedious as his verse. So try to believe me when I say I don't enjoy myself, quite as much as you imagine, and that I miss you more than I'd ever like to say at all those ' entertainments ' I'm forced to go to, and that there's Nothing quite like the company of one one loves to add real zest to life.'

CLITANDRE And now for me!

(reads) My dear Acaste

' Your little hanger-on Clitandre, who plays the lan-

64

guishing lover all the time, is the very last man on
earth I could feel real friendship for. He must be
out of his mind if he's convinced himself that I
feel anything at all for him; and you must be out
of yours to believe that I don't love you. Be reason-
able and take a leaf out of his book, and come and
see me as often as you can. That would be some
compensation for my having to be pestered by
Clitandre.'
This does your character enormous credit.
You really are a . . . No, I haven't said it!
We're going now and everywhere we call
we'll show this likeness of you, warts and all.

(Exit Clitandre)

ACASTE   I could say much. It's not worth the attempt.
You're quite beneath all anger and contempt.
Your ' little marquis ' certainly won't cry:
He's got far better fish than you to fry!

(Exit Acaste)

ORONTE   So after all those letters that you wrote
you turn on me like this and cut my throat!
You little gadabout, you seem to swear
undying, false devotion everywhere.
I've been a fool, but now the truth has dawned.
I'm grateful for the favour. I've been warned.
I've got my heart back and I'm glad to get it.
My only satisfaction 's *you* 'll regret it.
(to Alceste)
I'm thankful I've escaped this creature's claws.
I won't stand in your way. She's yours; all yours.

(Exit Oronte)

ARSINOE   O never have I felt so much disgust.
I'm shocked. I must speak out. I really must.
This fine and worthy man, Monsieur Alceste,
(I'm not so much concerned about the rest)

who worshipped you (to everyone's surprise)
Alceste, who thought the sun shone from your
eyes,
Alceste . . .

ALCESTE   I'll handle this if you don't mind
please don't waste your time in being kind
Crusading for my cause in this keen way
's not something I'd feel able to repay.
If, to avenge myself on Célimène,
you thing that I'll choose you, please think again.

ARSINOE What gave you the idea that I did?
As if I'd try to snare you! God forbid!
Such vanity! There's something monstrous in it,
if you can think such things a single minute.
This Madam's surplus stock 's a merchandise
I'd be an idiot to overprize.
Come down off your high horse before you fall.
My class of person 's not your type at all!
Dance attendance on that creature there.
You and that woman make a perfect pair!

(Exit Arsinoé)

ALCESTE I've waited in the wings all this long time
patiently watching this strange pantomime.
Have I proved my powers of self control
and may I now . . .

CELIMENE   Unburden your whole soul.
Yes, go on. I deserve all your complaint.
You're free to criticize without restraint.
I'm wrong and I admit it. Enough, enough,
no more pretending, no more lies and bluff.
I could despise the anger of the rest,
but you I know I've wronged, my poor Alceste.
Your resentment's justified. I realize
how culpable I must seem in your eyes.
All the evidence you've been given leads
to conclusive proof of my misdeeds.
There's every reason why you should detest

	me utterly. You have my leave, Alceste.
ALCESTE	Ah, you traitor, I only wish I could.
	If tenderness were crushable, I would.
	I want, I want to let myself give way
	to hate, but my heart just won't obey.
	(to Eliante and Philinte)
	Just how degrading can a passion get?
	Now watch me grovel. You've seen nothing yet.
	There's more to come. Just stay and watch the show.
	You'll see my weakness reach an all-time low.
	Never call men wise. Look how they behave.
	There's no perfection this side of the grave.
	(to Célimène)
	You've no idea what ' being faithful ' means . . .
	But I'm willing to forget these painful scenes,
	concoct excuses for your crimes and say
	the vicious times and youth led you astray,
	provided that, on your part, you consent
	to share my self-inflicted banishment,
	away, in the country, where I want to find
	a life-long haven and avoid mankind.
	In this way only, in the public eye,
	can you do penance for the injury
	those letters caused, and only if you do,
	can I pick up the threads of loving you.
CELIMENE	Renounce the world before I'm old and grey?
	Go to your wilderness and pine away?
ALCESTE	But if your love were anything like mine,
	you'd forget the outside world and never pine.
CELIMENE	I'm only twenty! I'd be terrified!
	Just you and me, and all that countryside!
	I'm not sufficiently high-minded to agree
	to such a fate. It's simply just not me!
	But if my hand's enough and you're content
	to marry and stay in Paris, I consent,
	and marriage . . .

ALCESTE   No, now I hate you, loathe, abhor.
This beats anything you've done before.
If you can't think of me as your whole life
as I would you, you'll never be my wife.
This last humiliation's set me free
from love's degrading tyranny.
(to Eliante)
To me you're beautiful, your virtue's clear.
and you're the only one who seems sincere.
I started to admire you long ago
and hope you'll let me go on doing so,
but, please, with all my troubles, understand
if now I hesitate to seek your hand.
I feel unworthy of it. It seems that Fate
didn't intend me for the married state.
Cast off by one not fit to lace your shoes,
my love's beneath your notice. You'd refuse.

ELIANTE Don't blame yourself, my friend. I understand.
I'm sure there'll be no problem with my hand.
I think a little pressure might persuade
your good friend here to volunteer his aid.

PHILINTE This makes my deepest wishes all come true.
I'd shirk no sacrifice in serving you.

ALCESTE I hope you'll always feel so, and both win
a joy and happiness that's genuine.
For me, betrayed on all sides and laid low
by heaped injustices, it's time to go,
and leave man floundering in this foul morass
where vice goes swaggering as bold as brass,
and go on looking for a safe retreat
where honesty can stand on its own feet.

(Exit Alceste)

PHILINTE Let's go after him, and see if we can't find
some way (*any* way!) to change his mind.

(Exeunt Philinte and Eliante together. Célimène remains seated, alone she laughs, then falls silent, rises, crosses to the window, and stares out.)

68

CELIMENE: but what I *do* find difficult to do
's announce my choice in front of both of you.   (*Act III, p. 61*)

CELIMENE (Diana Rigg) ORONTE (Gawn Grainger) ALCESTE (Alec McCowen)

ACASTE: As for the little Marquis *(that's me, gentlemen, though, I shouldn't boast)* ... As for the little Marquis, who held my hand so interminably yesterday, he's of no account at all, absolutely insignificant, a tailor's dummy, that's all the little Marquis is.　　　　　　　　　　*(Act III, p. 64)*

left to right, CELIMENE (Diana Rigg) PHILINTE (Alan MacNaughtan) ARSINOE (Gillian Barge) CLITANDRE (Jeremy Clyde) ACASTE (Nicholas Clay) ORONTE (Gawn Grainger) ELIANTE (Jeanne Watts) ALCESTE (Alec McCowen)

ALCESTE: But if your love were anything like mine,
          you'd forget the outside world and never pine.   (*Act III, p. 67*)

CELIMENE (Diana Rigg) ALCESTE (Alec McCowen) PHILINTE (Alan MacNaughtan)

PHILINTE: This makes my deepest wishes all come true.
           I'd shirk no sacrifice in serving you.   (*Act III, p. 68*)

CELIMENE (Diana Rigg)   PHILINTE (Alan MacNaughton)   ELIANTE (Jeanne Watts)